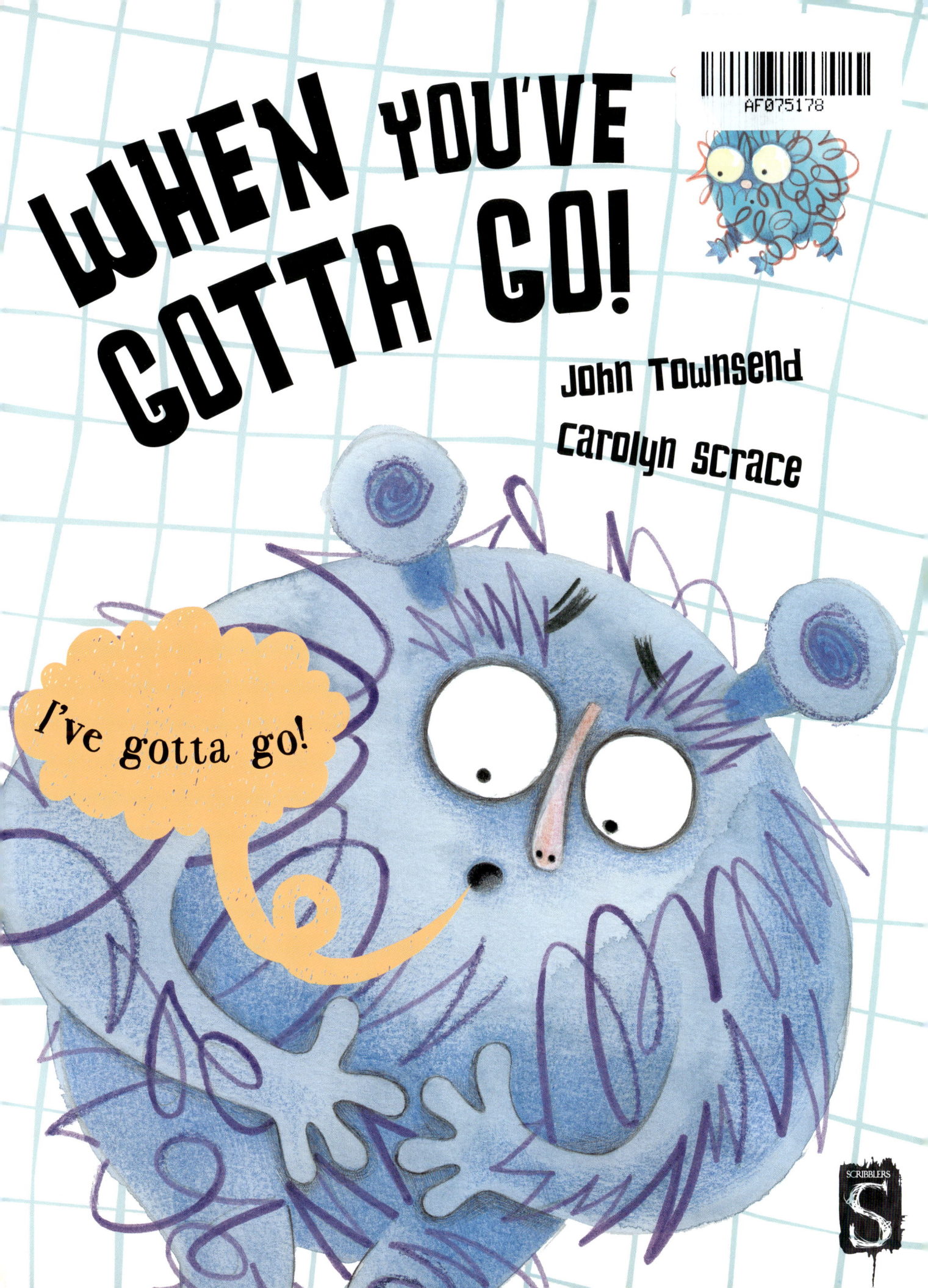

Published in Great Britain in MMXXI by Scribblers, an imprint of
The Salariya Book Company Ltd
25 Marlborough Place, Brighton BN1 1UB
www.salariya.com

ISBN: 978-1-913337-92-6

SALARIYA
SCRIBO BOOK HOUSE SCRIBBLERS

© The Salariya Book Company Ltd MMXXI
All rights reserved. No part of this publication may be reproduced, stored in or introduced into a retrieval system or transmitted in any form, or by any means (electronic, mechanical, photocopying, recording or otherwise) without the written permission of the publisher. Any person who does any unauthorised act in relation to this publication may be liable to criminal prosecution and civil claims for damages.

1 3 5 7 9 8 6 4 2

A CIP catalogue record for this book is available from the British Library.

This book is sold subject to the conditions that it shall not, by way of trade or otherwise, be lent, resold, hired out, or otherwise circulated without the publisher's prior consent in any form or binding or cover other than that in which it is published and without similar condition being imposed on the subsequent purchaser.

Editor: Nick Pierce

Visit
www.salariya.com
for our online catalogue and
free fun stuff.

PAPER FROM SUSTAINABLE FORESTS

No need to blush, just use the flush!

Don't be grotty with a potty!

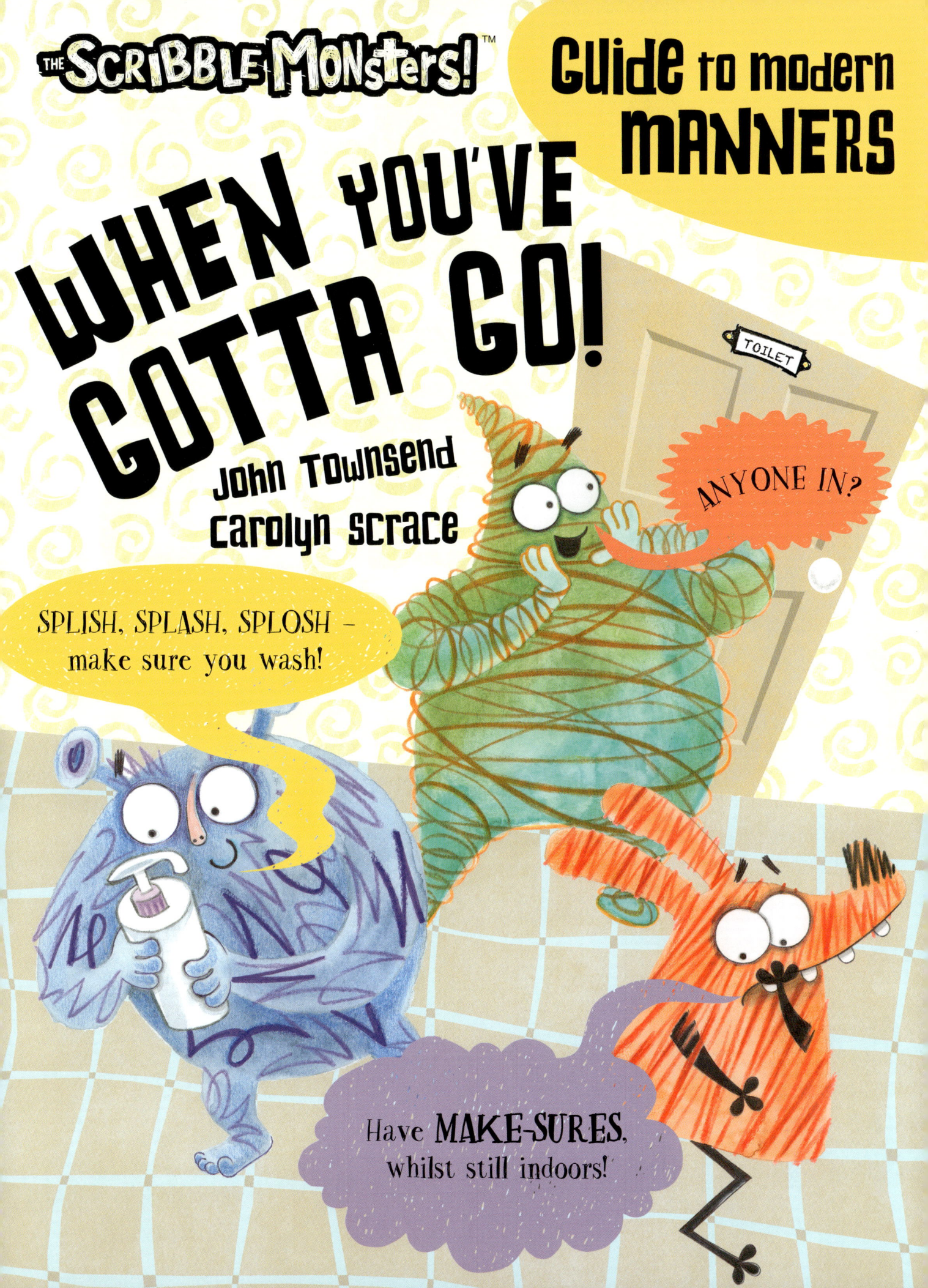

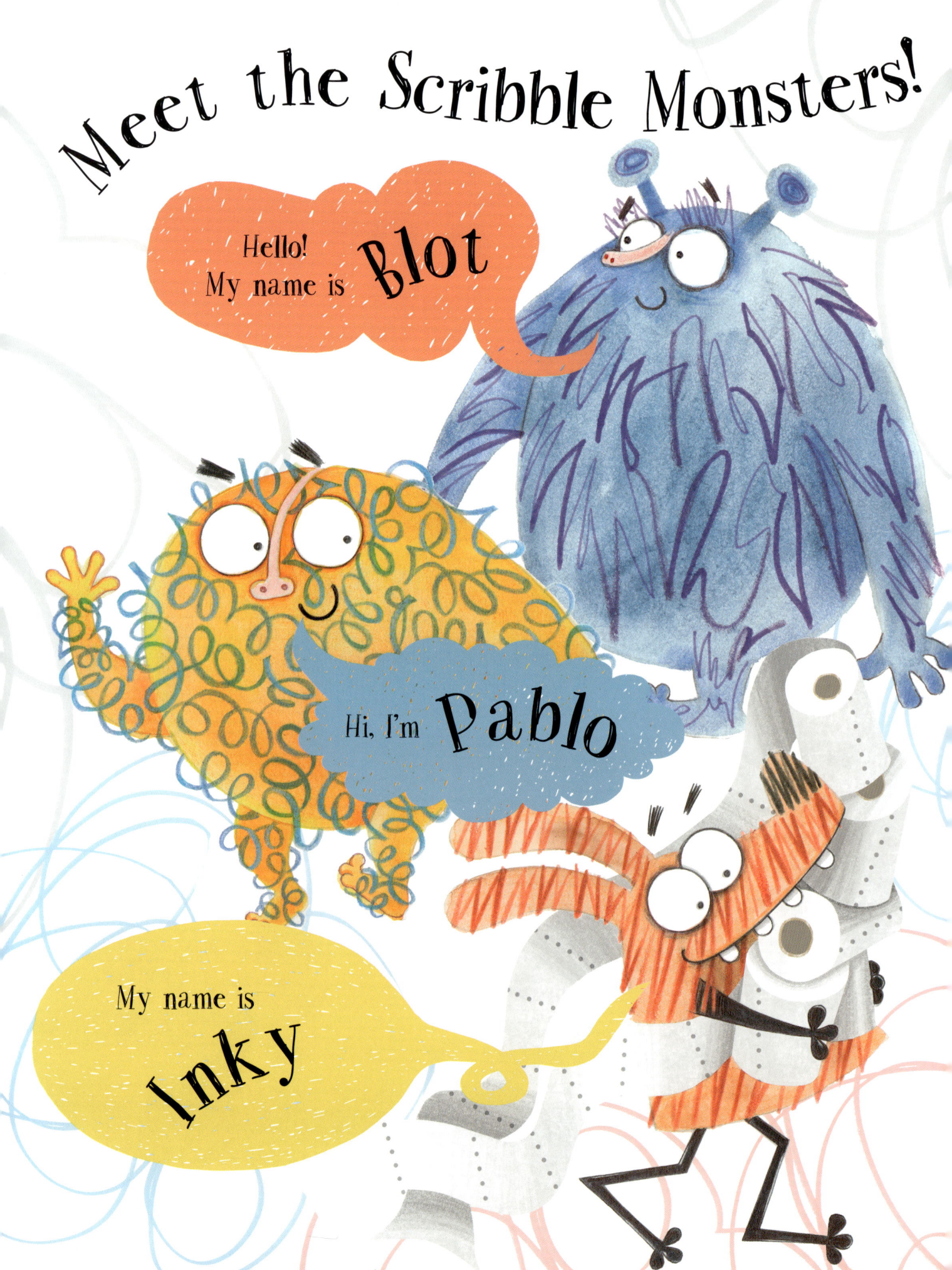

Some little children can forget
To tidy up behind them.
We're here to scribble our advice
And find ways to remind them.

Smudge tells a little puppy friend,

You must be tidy, Spotty.
Please sit still, try not to splash
Each time you are on the potty.

The Scribble Monsters give awards
To children who say 'YES'
To manners when it's potty time...

You're a **Potty Star Success!**

If you need to use a potty,
Make sure you're quick, don't wait...
Otherwise, if you delay
You might just be too late.

Make **sure** you go before a trip,
Just think ahead and judge,
To stop a little accident...
'Like I once had,' says Smudge.

Vroom Vroom

When Pablo was a little lad
He had a nasty habit:
He never touched the toilet's flush –
He didn't want to grab it!

Here's Inky with some good advice
From when things once went wrong:

I went outside to play for hours
And left it far too long!

The toilet was too far away,

And I was far too busy.

But then a little accident
Put Inky in a tizzy!

H.B. gives advice most mornings
When Blot gets in a muddle...
He sometimes doesn't aim too well,
Then leaves a little puddle.

After using any toilet
Or any potty, too,
Nibs says:

Always wash your hands,
That's the healthy thing to do.

CAN YOU HELP US FIND THE ANSWERS TO THIS QUIZ?

QUESTION 1

When I'm on the potty, should I sit still and try not to splash?

QUESTION 2

Should we have a **make-sure** before we go out?

QUESTION 3

After we use any toilet or potty, what should we do with the toilet roll?

QUESTION 4

What is the golden rule when we go into the toilet?

Look at the last page of the book to see if you are right!

MORE MONSTER QUESTIONS

QUESTION 5

When we're done, should we take our time and flush the toilet?

QUESTION 6

When we need to use the potty, should we aim to the side?

QUESTION 7

After we use any toilet or potty, what should we do to our hands?

QUESTION 8

Before we leave the bathroom we must do what?

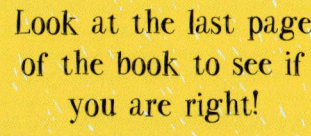

Look at the last page of the book to see if you are right!

GOODBYE!

Goodbye!

Goodbye!

Goodbye!

Goodbye!

Goodbye!

Answers to the quiz:
1. Yes!
2. Yes!
3. Wipe yourself a lot.
4. Close the door before you start.
5. Yes!
6. No! Aim into the middle.
7. Always wash them.
8. Pull up our pants and zip.